D0475530

MR. TANEN'S Tie TROUBLE

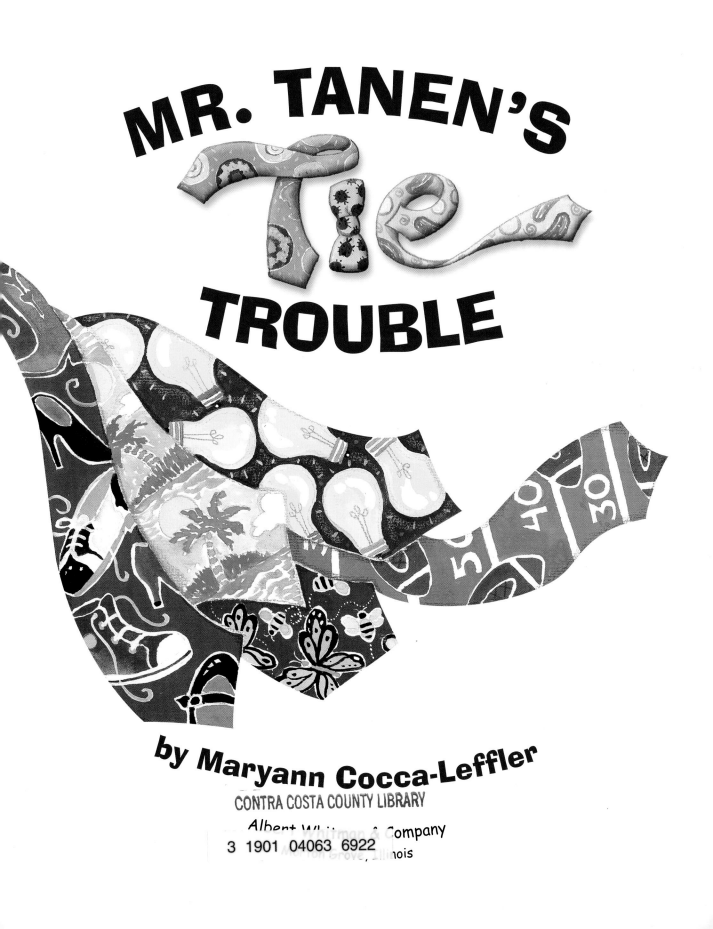

by Maryann Cocca-Leffler

Albert Whitman & Company
Morton Grove, Illinois

To my editor, Abby Levine.
Thank you from the
bottom of my tie!

Library of Congress Cataloging-in-
Publication Data

Cocca-Leffler, Maryann, 1958-
Mr. Tanen's tie trouble / written and
illustrated by Maryann Cocca-Leffler.
p. cm.
Summary: Mr. Tanen loves his ties, but when
his school runs out of money to build a new
playground, he decides to sell his ties in order to
raise the needed money.
ISBN 0-8075-5305-0 (hardcover)
[1. School principals—Fiction. 2. Neckties—Fiction.
3. Generosity—Fiction.]   I. Title.
PZ7.C638Mp 2003
[E]—dc21
2002011329

For more information about Albert Whitman & Company,
visit our web site at www.albertwhitman.com.

Please visit Maryann Cocca-Leffler at her web site:
www.maryanncoccaleffler.com.

It was very early when Mr. Tanen unlocked the door to the school. He had a lot to do. This was the first day back after winter vacation. As principal of the Lynnhurst School, his job was to get everything ready before the children arrived.

NO CLIMBING

CLOSED FOR REPAIRS

Bijou BAKERY

He clicked on all the classroom lights,

"Ohhh, fresh paint!"

turned up the heat,

"Ahhh, nice and warm at last!"

and stocked the refrigerator with milk.

"Brrr, the fridge is fixed!"

Finally he entered his office. He opened his closet door and smiled.

TIES...lots of ties, tumbled out!

Mr. Tanen was known and loved for his wild and crazy tie collection. He had 975 ties! He wore a different one for every occasion, activity, or mood.

He slipped on his new Doughnut and Danish Tie and poured himself a cup of coffee.

Mr. Tanen arranged his ties for the day: the Back-to-Jail Tie for the teachers' meeting, the School Bus Tie to greet the kids, and the Pizza Tie for lunch.

Then he searched until he found the Swing and Slide Tie. He was very excited. Today he would announce that the school had saved enough money to install a wonderful new playground! The children deserved it. They had collected cans and held bake sales to add money to the playground fund.

RRRINGG

Just then, the phone rang. It was Mr. Apple from the School Department.

"Mr. Tanen, welcome back!" said Mr. Apple. "I've been working on the school budget. Everything that needed fixing was fixed over vacation."

"I've been noticing all morning," said Mr. Tanen. "Fresh paint, steaming heat, and a cold refrigerator! Thank you so much, Mr. Apple!"

"Don't thank me yet!" said Mr. Apple. "I just received the bills. We are out of money! The playground will have to wait."

"OH, NO, Mr. Apple! Can't you find the money somewhere else?" begged Mr. Tanen. "What am I going to tell the kids?"

"You'll think of something," said Mr. Apple softly. "I'm sorry, Mr. Tanen. I wish I could tell you that our bank account is as full as your tie closet!"

Mr. Tanen sadly hung up the phone and gazed out at the broken-down playground. He heard a *clink-clank*. He looked up to see Kaylee and Alex lugging in a big jar filled with money.

"Here it is! $148.29 for the playground fund!" said Kaylee proudly.

"New playground, here we come!" cheered Alex.

Mr. Tanen didn't know what to say.

After school, Mr. Tanen sat in his office staring at the jar. He sighed. "Now I'm in a real pickle! This is not enough money for a playground. The kids will be so disappointed." Mr. Apple's words floated around in his head:

"The playground will have to wait."

"You'll think of something."

"I wish our bank account was as full as your tie closet."

"Hmm . . . as full as my tie closet!" repeated Mr. Tanen.

He jumped up, opened his closet, and shouted, "That's IT! MY TIES! Lynnhurst School WILL have a new playground!"

The next day, the entire town was plastered with signs.

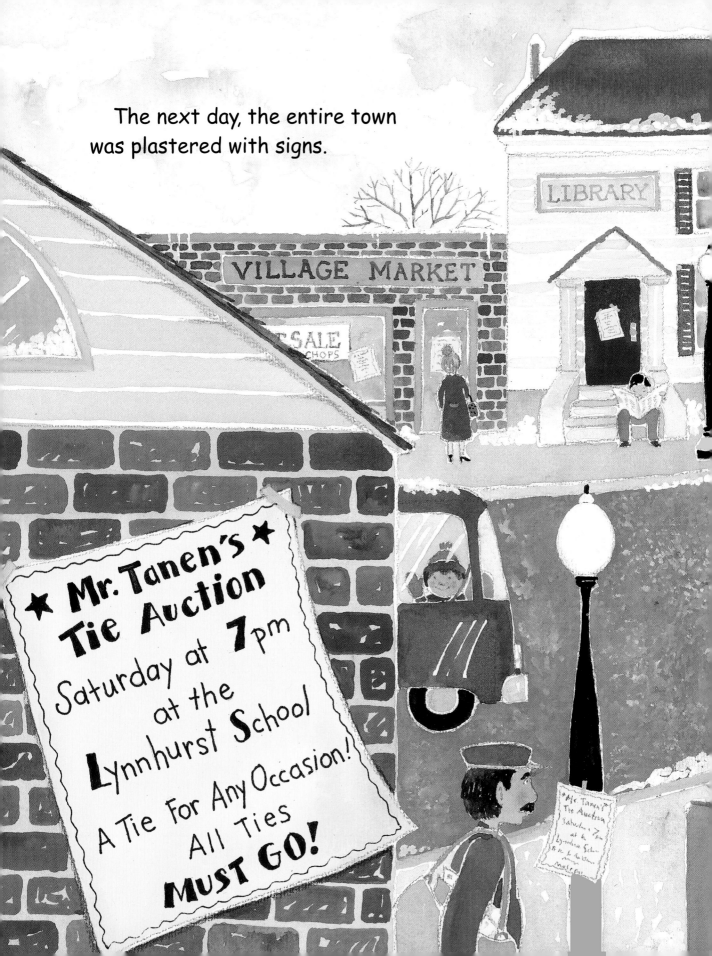

LIBRARY

VILLAGE MARKET

SALE
CHOPS

★ Mr. Tanen's ★
Tie Auction
Saturday at 7pm
at the
Lynnhurst School
A Tie For Any Occasion!
All Ties
MUST GO!

Mrs. Sweet Apple noticed the sign on the grocery store window. She called her husband, Mr. Apple.

"Why is Mr. Tanen selling all his ties? Has he gone crazy?"

Mr. Apple told her about the school budget and the playground money. The town was buzzing all day . . .

Mrs. Sweet Apple called Monsieur Bijou at the bakery,

who called Cleo at the cleaners,

who called Dr. Demi the dentist . . .

It went on and on, until even Zack, the night watchman at the zoo, got the word:

"Mr. Tanen is selling his ties!"

On Saturday, the whole town showed up for the auction. Monsieur Bijou started the bidding. "I'll give you $50 for the Doughnut and Danish Tie!"

Lolly the librarian bought the Book Tie.

Dr. Demi was the proud new owner of the Toothbrush Tie.

Kaylee handed over her entire piggy bank for the Hot Dog Tie.

Mrs. Sweet Apple just had to have the Wedding Bells Tie, and of course, Mr. Apple chuckled as he paid quite a bit of cash for the Crabapple Tie.

* Mr. Tanen's *
Tie Auction
Saturday at 7pm
at the
Lynnhurst School
A Tie For My Graduation
All Ties
MUST GO!

The auction was a huge success! Every tie was sold, except one. Mr. Tanen couldn't part with his beloved Blue Ribbon Tie. It was a present from Mr. Apple for being a great principal. He looked out at a sea of townspeople, all wearing his ties.

"Thank you all. I have always taught my students, 'The more you give, the more you get.' With this money, the Lynnhurst School will have a new playground!"

Mr. Tanen swallowed hard. "My ties now belong to the town. Wear them proudly."

And throughout the spring, that's just what everyone did.

But sometimes Mr. Tanen would forget his closet was empty. He would open it to get a tie, and with a tinge of sadness, he would remember. He only had one tie—and he was wearing it. Then he'd look outside at the playground being built.

"You have to give to get," he thought.

Soon it was Opening Day at the new playground. Mr. Tanen had invited the whole town to the ribbon-cutting ceremony. He tucked his speech in his pocket, grabbed his special scissors, and adjusted his tie. He wished he had on his official Ribbon-Cutting Tie.

The schoolyard was overflowing with people.
Mr. Tanen made his way through the crowd.

Then he saw it!

Mr. Tanen's Playground

The playground was tied in a giant
ribbon made from Mr. Tanen's ties!

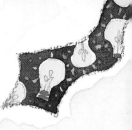

Mrs. Sweet Apple and Mr. Apple were at the microphone.

"Mr. Tanen, you have taught us all, 'The more you give, the more you get,'" said Mrs. Sweet Apple. "You have given us a playground. We are giving you back your ties."

With that, Mr. Apple untied
the tie ribbon and announced:
"Mr. Tanen's Playground is

NOW OPEN!"

Mr. Tanen and his ties
were together again!
He slipped on his Swing
and Slide Tie and smiled.